Thai Children's
Favorite Stories

Thai Children's
Favorite Stories

FABLES, MYTHS, LEGENDS AND FAIRY TALES

Written by Marian D. Toth

Illustrated by Patcharee Meesukhon

TUTTLE Publishing

Tokyo | Rutland, Vermont | Singapore

Contents

How the Bay of Bangkok Came to Be   6

Why Do We Have Thunder and Lightning?   14

How the Thais Learned to Be Calm   18

The Gold Harvest   24

Princess Golden Flower and the Vulture King   32

The Wisest Man in Siam   38

There Is No Such Thing As a Secret   45

How the Tiger Got Its Stripes   50

The Footprint of the Buddha   56

Glossary   62

How the Bay of Bangkok Came to Be

Once upon a time a kite flew above yellow bamboo rooftops, past green jungles, and high into the bright blue sky of Thailand. During the day it blocked the sun and at night it hid the moon. This kite was larger than an elephant, larger than a house. It was the largest kite in Thailand and maybe the largest kite in the world.

If you slid from the kite through the clouds, down the long yellow kite string, you would find yourself in the compound of Khun Keha, the best kite maker in Thailand. He was an old man but he always felt young when kites were flying. During the third month, the mango monsoons blew like gusts from a giant bamboo fan. The largest kite in Thailand needed strong winds to keep it flying. Khun Keha prayed to the gods to encourage the winds to blow. He had spent over a year making his gigantic masterpiece and now he wanted all the children in his village to enjoy it.

The idea for the kite came in the Year of the Snake on a day when Khun Keha's compound hummed with the busy noises of children making kites. Sawdust puffed into the air like the pollen of flowers. Paint brushes swished reds, blues and yellows over slender strips of

6

bamboo. Khun Keha could not take a step without meeting a question.

"Is it true that kites can call the winds and bring rain to the rice field, Khun Keha?"

"Chai, it is so. Kites can even tell what will happen in the future. Some wise men look at a flying kite and see in each movement a glimpse of things to come."

"Can kites do anything else, Khun Keha?"

"Chai," he answered. "Sometimes we use them to carry explosives. Kites are also good soldiers."

"Khun Keha, can a man ride in a kite?" asked a child.

Khun Keha paused and shook his head. "Mai ruu, I don't know. No one has tried it. I guess a man would need a kite as big as a house to ride in it."

"Can you build a kite that big?" they asked.

Khun Keha laughed. "I don't know, but I can try. Will you help me?"

The children shouted, "Chai!" and shrieked with delight.

"Run along now, children. You must rest now. Tomorrow we will watch the kite fights."

The next day Khun Keha took his little friends to watch the kite fights in front of the king's royal palace. "Watch carefully, children, the kites are like boys and girls quarreling. The male kites are called chula. They are big and star shaped. The female kites are called pakpao. They are small and dainty.

"Kite fighting is a team sport. The object is to keep your kite in the air and guide it to attack the enemy kites. Both the chula and the pakpao try to force each other out of the sky."

After the kite fight he took the children home and taught them how to make chula and pakpao kites. His compound was full of the laughter of happy children.

"Where do I place the hooks on my chula kite?" a little boy asked.

"Put the hooks on the bottom so they can catch the strings of the pakpao," he said.

The little girls said, "Khun Keha, you want the chula kites to win! Come, help us with our pakpao kites."

"Now, children," said Khun Keha. "It isn't who wins that matters. It is how well you observe the rules of the game. In kite fighting there are fifty rules to remember. It takes a long time to learn them. Most of all, you must be as clever as a tiger to make your pakpao twist and dip. Each flutter of wind sends the pakpao in a different direction. The pakpao is like a chicken chased by a dog. You never know which way the chicken will go."

"Chula kites are stronger," said the boys.

"Chai," said Khun Keha.

The little boys gathered around Khun Keha and said, "Khun Keha, why don't you make a chula kite that is bigger than a house?"

"We shall see, we shall see," he said.

When the kite season was over, Khun Keha began to make an enormous chula kite. It was so long he had to remove the end of his house. It was so tall, he had to remove the ceiling from his house. To add the sides, he had to tear down the rest of the house. Poor Khun Keha did not have a house any more but he had a giant kite. It was the only kite in Thailand bigger than a house.

Every day the children came to watch Khun Keha paint swirls, diamonds and traditional designs on the kite. They agreed it was not only the largest but also the most beautiful kite in Thailand.

   On the first day of the waning
moon, the wind roared across the ocean
and swept over the jungles. It was a strong
and steady wind. Before the sun dawned, all
the children gathered next to Khun Keha's kite.
They greeted their friend by clasping both hands
together, bowing their heads and saying, "Sawaddi,
good morning, Khun Keha. Please may we fly the
kite today?"

   Khun Keha smiled. "When a baby stands alone,
we say he is setting up the egg. Today let us set up
the egg for our kite and let it fly for the first time."

   Khun Keha called eight of the larger children
and gave each a heavy rope that was attached to the kite. He pulled the
first rope himself. After a brief moment, no longer than
it takes a chingchok lizard to catch a fly, the kite stirred
to life. It soared into the sky like a giant bird. Higher and
higher it flew while the children cheered and shouted.

   Khun Keha tied the long guide rope to a huge boulder. He spent
the rest of the day preparing a surprise for the children. It was a sliding
pulley that allowed them to ride from the ground through the sky to the
giant chula kite.

The children's faces brimmed with wonder as they floated in the kite with old Khun Keha. It was like being in a magical world. All around them were soft white clouds fleeced with silver. The only sound was the flap of a bird's wing or the whistle of the wind. At this great height the wind only tickled the kite and made it sway like a swing. Far below, the earth seemed as neat as a chessboard with rice paddies in squares. The network of klong canals looked like silver footpaths. All the houses looked the same, like little boxes on stilts.

Each day during kite season the children dashed home from school, then met Khun Keha in the clouds. He told them stories and gave them coconut candy. If he had not done these kind things, they still would have come because the greatest joy of all was to observe the beauty of the world from the kite in the sky.

One day the clouds were dark and the skies were scowling. "A great storm is coming," said Khun Keha. "You may not go up to the kite today."

As he spoke, a harsh wind almost blew the children off their feet. The kite began to sway and its rock anchor moved slightly. "I'm afraid our kite may be damaged in this storm. Let's bring it down."

Khun Keha and all the children pulled on the sturdy rope, but the force of the wind was so great that it lifted them from the ground. "Rawang! Rawang! Be careful, children. We must let the kite go!"

The children obeyed, and just at that moment a powerful gust of wind carried their enormous kite high into the sky, so it quickly disappeared from view. Khun Keha sent the children home while he prayed for the gods to return his kite.

What happened to the beautiful kite, the largest kite in Thailand? We shall never know for certain, but the people who live in the south say that long ago a kite bigger than a house whirled through the sky, fell with a crash, tore open the earth, and created the Bay of Bangkok.

Now Khun Keha did not have a house and he did not have a kite. But he had the honor of changing the geography of his country, and he had the love of all the children in the land. He considered himself a wealthy man.

Why Do We Have Thunder and Lightning?

When lightning flashes and thunder roars, Thai mothers say, "Don't be afraid, children. It's only Mekhala flashing her crystal ball. She is teasing the cruel god of thunder, Ramasura."

Mekhala is a beautiful Thai goddess with sparkling black eyes and shining black hair. It is said she was born in the foam of the sea. She is the goddess of the streams, rivers and oceans of the world.

Ramasura is a demigod, half ogre and half divine and he carries a beautiful ax decorated with diamonds. He was born in a storm cloud, and to this day he wears a rain cloud as a cloak.

All the gods and goddesses are fond of Mekhala because of her happy, carefree manner. They delight in watching her tease those who are serious. Her favorite victim is Ramasura. He is not a popular god because, it is said, he is harsh, cruel and violent. Worst of all, he has a very bad habit of throwing his ax at those who offend him.

Fortunately, Ramasura and Mekhala don't meet often. Most of the year Mekhala stays in the palace of her husband, Siva, where she spends her time polishing her crystal ball.

Mekhala's father had given her the crystal ball when she had married the great god Siva. "Now Mekhala, you must be a good wife to Siva," he said. "My wedding gift to you is a sparkling crystal ball. It will amuse you and keep you occupied. You must always keep it polished, my child."

"Chai," said Mekhala. "I shall do as you say, Father."

She kept her word, polishing her crystal ball until it sparkled like a brilliant star. But polishing the crystal was Mekhala's only task, and soon she became bored with her work.

"If I only had someone to talk to," she sighed. "I do wish Siva would not leave me alone in this beautiful palace."

One day, when the monsoon season began, the gods and goddesses assembled in heaven to celebrate the life-giving gift of rain. They sang and danced as happily as mortals. As it was such a special occasion, Siva allowed Mekhala to attend the party. When she arrived, everyone stopped dancing and looked at her sparkling eyes, shining hair and her beautiful crystal ball that flashed beams of light into the sky.

When Ramasura saw the beautiful Mekhala he walked toward her. She flashed her jewel in his eyes and laughed at the huge god.

"Don't you know who I am?" he roared.

Mekhala giggled and flew in and out of the fluffy clouds.

The winds whipped through the sky as Ramasura tried to find Mekhala. Most goddesses would have been terrified but Mekhala thought it was great fun to hide in the clouds and flash her crystal ball at Ramasura. She led him all over heaven as she skipped and giggled, diving into clouds and hiding in their mists.

The more she laughed, the more enraged Ramasura became. "I'll catch that little teaser if it is the last thing I do," he said.

No one could catch a goddess who darted as fast as a ray of sunlight, and it seemed as if Mekhala had escaped. Then, suddenly, Ramasura raised his arm and aimed his glittering ax at her. She flashed her crystal in his eyes and blinded him just as the ax flew from his hand with a thunderous sound. Again and again he hurled his ax at her, but his aim was always spoiled by the light from her crystal.

On a stormy night, look into the sky. That flash of lightning is the sparkle of Mekhala's crystal ball. The roar of thunder is Ramasura's ax rolling across the corridors of the sky. If you sit very still and listen carefully you may hear Mekhala's tinkling laughter, and if the clouds should part suddenly, you may see a graceful goddess darting above the mists with a sparkling crystal ball flashing rays of brilliant light into Ramasura's angry eyes.

16

How the Thais Learned to Be Calm

Once there was a quiet, sleepy village. It was called Peaceful Village because everyone who lived there said, "My neighbor is my friend." The people worked together each season of the year, in the rain, in the heat, in the dry season. They were always together like bunches of bananas in a tree. Then a terrible thing happened, as quick and unexpected as a flash of lightning in the sky. Peace left the village and these loving neighbors became enemies.

It happened one day long ago when the red sun burned over the horizon and shone on the bamboo huts in Peaceful Village. The roosters crowed, as they always did, and stretched their wings like unfolding fans. The pigs oinked and poked their noses in the earth. The rice farmers washed the sleep from their eyes, rinsed their mouths with water, and chewed a wad of betel nut before going to work in the paddy. The women put yokes on the water buffaloes and woke their sleepy sons. The boys rode on the backs of the buffaloes and guided them to the paddy.

That morning a little chingchok lizard, no bigger than a mouse, slithered onto the dirt road running through Peaceful Village. Its brown body looked like a drop of mud slung from the hoof of a buffalo. The farmers and their sons passed the chingchok on the way to the paddy. The shopkeeper's sons skipped by it on their way to the wat where they recited their lesson for the priest. No one paid any attention to the chingchok because others just like him were in the houses, the trees and the compounds of every Thai family.

The chingchok fell fast asleep by the side of the road. Nothing disturbed him, not even a little boy carrying a big pot of honey. As the boy skipped down the road, his pot rocked from side to side and a golden drop of honey flew through the air, landing on the sand beside the sleeping chingchok.

This day, long ago, seemed like any other day. The lizard slept, the drop of honey sparkled in the sun, and the housewives went on with their work. They cooked the morning rice, scooped it onto banana leaves, and wrapped it with string, like a present. The children carried the little green bundles to their fathers in the paddy. Some wives mashed rice into flour with mortar and pestle. Others wove cotton threads into fabric on

large handlooms. In one compound, not far from the sleeping
chingchok, a woman and her friend sang a little baby to
sleep in a cradle.

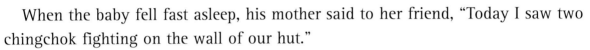

> *It's twelve o'clock my baby,*
> *The turtle dove is still;*
> *He cries from dawn to noon time*
> *But now his voice is still.*
> *And you must rest, my baby,*
> *For the sun is past the hill.*

When the baby fell fast asleep, his mother said to her friend, "Today I saw two
chingchok fighting on the wall of our hut."

"It is an omen of evil. It means your family will suffer illness and maybe death,"
said the woman as her face wrinkled into a worried frown. "You must offer rice to the
guardian spirit of your place. If you burn incense for him and bring him fresh flowers, he
may keep the evil from falling upon you."

Two little children, a boy and a girl, listened to their mothers' conversation.

"Run along, little rat, run along, little rabbit," the mothers said to them. The children
skipped down the road arm in arm.

"My mother is terribly worried because the chingchok were fighting on the wall of
our house this morning," said the little girl.

As they passed the sleeping chingchok, the little girl said, "Look, this chingchok is
sleeping just an elephant's step away from my cat."

"And my dog is sleeping in the shade behind your cat," said the little boy.

Just then the chingchok opened his beady eyes. The first thing he saw was the drop of honey gleaming in the sunlight. With a fast dart and one quick lick of his tongue he devoured the honey. The scurrying of the chingchok alerted the cat. She caught him with her paw and rolled him over in the sand. The scuffle awakened the dog. He snarled and barked at the cat. She arched her back and hissed like the fuse on a firecracker. The dog growled fiercely. The girl grabbed a stick and beat the growling dog. "Don't you dare hurt my cat," she said. The little boy began to beat the little girl and he shouted, "Don't you dare hurt my dog!"

The girl's mother came running to the scene. She slapped the boy and screamed, "Don't you dare hurt my little girl."

The boy's mother heard him cry and rushed to the street. "You beast," she yelled. "Don't you dare hurt my little boy."

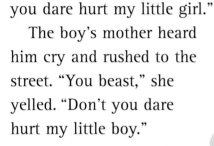

Friends of both women came running. When they heard the story, they started to fight, throwing sticks and stones and shouting insults. The women even pointed their toes at their enemies' heads. Nothing was more insulting than this. The shouting disturbed the ricebirds. They fluttered above the paddies, darkening the sky with their flapping wings.

The farmers heard the scream of a child, the sob of a mother, a wild shout, and an angry roaring of voices. They did not stop to unyoke their buffaloes and let them have an afternoon rest. They did not check their fishing nets and bring home the day's catch. They did not sit on their buffaloes' backs and play their bamboo flutes as the animals plodded homeward. The startled men dropped their plowshares and came running.

By the time the rice farmers reached the village, the drop of honey, the lizard, the cat, the dog, and the two quarreling children were forgotten. Each man tried to defend his wife and soon found himself furiously fighting his friends and brothers.

The next day the villagers found themselves divided into two camps. Each side dug trenches, and built barricades. For twenty days and twenty nights they fought each other. Brothers killed brothers and fathers killed sons in a meaningless war.

The streets of the village became littered with trash and the houses became dirty and unswept. Weeds choked the rice plants. The water buffaloes' skin cracked because no one gave them their daily bath. As the days passed it was clear that no one was winning but no one was willing to give up.

Soon the king heard the shocking news that Peaceful Village was at war. He immediately ordered soldiers to quiet the warring village. The villagers were angry that

the king was interfering and joined together in an effort to keep the king's soldiers away. After many days and many deaths the village became as still as the jungle at dawn. When all was quiet, the king's soldiers departed. It is said the people in the village felt shame and sorrow.

"How foolish we were," the people said.

"This must never happen again," said the village elders.

"Let us learn from the experience and be calm forever more," said the village priests.

It is said, from that time onward, the Thai people have been calm and even-tempered. Their children are taught to be gentle and well mannered, but occasionally, like children everywhere, they are headstrong and act without thinking. Whenever this happens, Thai mothers tell their children about the honey, the lizard, the cat, the dog, and the two quarreling children who started the war in Peaceful Village.

The Gold Harvest

Long ago in old Ayudhya there lived a man named Nai Hah Tong who dreamed of turning copper into gold. His wife, Nang Song Sai, had little faith in magic. When her husband boasted, "Some day we will be the richest people in Ayudhya," she listened patiently but when all their money had been used for his experiments, she decided something would have to be done.

"Nai Hah Tong," she said, "you've experimented with copper and a monkey's paw, copper and a lizard's tail. You've polished copper with a golden stripe of tiger fur, but the copper did not turn into gold. Why don't you give up and go to work like other men?"

Her husband said, "Mai chai, that is not right. With each experiment my magic has grown stronger."

"Mai pen rai, never mind, my husband, you must do what you must do," she answered.

The next day, however, she went home to ask her father for advice. Her wise old father

24

did not seem disturbed. He said, "Pai, go now, and say nothing of this meeting. I have a plan to help your husband."

Next day Nai Hah Tong received an invitation to dine with his father-in-law. They sat together on the mat-covered floor and the old man said, "My son, since you desire power and a long life, you sit facing east. I seek honor and dignity, so I shall sit facing west."

"Chai, yes, my father. I always follow the old belief. I never sit facing north when I eat, for I fear the bad luck that would bring, but sometimes I eat facing south because I want people to respect me." The old man smiled and nodded in agreement.

A servant brought in a large tray bearing bowls of white rice, hot chicken curry, eggs, vegetables, and namprik, a spicy sauce made from beetles and fish paste. Another tray held bowls of fresh water, cloths, and lime scent, for washing, drying, and perfuming the hands. The men ate from the same bowls, using only the fingers of their right hand. They did not speak much while eating because the delicious food demanded their complete attention. The curry was spicy, yet sweet with coconut milk. The rice was fluffy and fresh from the top of the pot. The namprik bit the tongue, but it was good and made the mild coconut milk drink more tasty by contrast.

When the meal was over, Nai Hah Tong felt as content as a baby gibbon sitting upon his mother's lap.

"Ah, we are lucky to have fish in the water and rice on the land," he said.

"Chai, my son, but there is more to life than good food. I have asked you to come to see me this evening because I need your help. Like you, my son, I have been looking for a way of turning copper into gold. Now, I know how to do it."

Nai Hah Tong drew in his breath and made a long, low whistling sound. "Oh, it's too good to be true! I can't believe it!" he said.

"Listen carefully, Nai Hah Tong. I have all I need for the miracle except one thing. Because I am an old man, I don't think I can work hard enough or long enough to get it."

"Mai pen rai, don't worry, Father. I will get whatever you need." Nai Hah Tong replied.

"That is not as easy as you might think, my son. I must have two kilos of soft fuzz gathered from the underside of the banana leaf, and the fuzz must be plucked carefully from your very own banana trees. Furthermore, I know the fuzz will not perform the miracle, unless it comes from a tree planted when magical words are spoken."

"I can say the magic words and I can raise the bananas. I will collect the two kilos of banana fuzz for you," said Nai Hah Tong.

The old man smiled and said, "I know you can do this, my son. Because I have faith in you, I will loan you the money to buy the land you will need to raise banana trees."

The young man bowed low to the elder. In the hearts of each of them there was a feeling of faith and trust.

Nai Hah Tong was determined to prepare his fields in a way which would be most pleasing to all the gods who could help his crops to grow. So he went to his village wat and asked guidance from the monk who knew how to tell the future by looking at the stars. The monk's bare feet made no sound as he walked from the wat to the open courtyard. His saffron robe glowed in the moonlight. The monk gazed at the glittering

stars that lit the sky like fireflies while Nai Hah Tong waited. The only sound was the call of a gecko lizard hiding in a crack of the wall of the wat. He counted the lizard's croaks: nung, sawng, sam, see, ha, hok, jet. One, two, three, four, five, six, seven.

"Ah, it is a rare sign of good fortune. The gecko calls seven times, bringing good luck."

The monk returned to his small, bare cell and opened a worn folding book. He said, "Since you were born in the Year of the Ox, you must begin your plowing on Wednesday, the tenth day of the fourth lunar month. Now, do not forget to begin when the sun is midway between the horizon and the highpoint of noon."

"Chai, chai, yes, yes. I shall do as you say."

"But first you must build a shrine to the guardian spirit of the field, Phra Phum. Give him an offering of the best rice. Lay it flat on a shining green banana leaf and serve him graciously. At the north corner of your field you must place three triangular white flags. As you mount them on bamboo poles, ask the blessing of the goddess who makes the banana tree rich with yellow fruit. Do not forget to praise the Earth Goddess and do remember to ask Phra Phum's blessing. Ask these gods to keep hungry locusts and nibbling worms far away from your fields."

"Is there anything else that I must do?" asked Nai Hah Tong.

"Chai, you will ask your village chieftain to guide your plow three times around the field. When this is done, again honor Phra Phum with the scent of incense and the beauty of flowers plucked by your own hands."

Nai Hah Tong followed the monk's suggestions and with the planting of each banana tree he said the special secret words given to him by his father-in-law. His banana trees grew tall, sturdy and heavy with blossoms. Soon he had thousands of firm yellow bananas and a myriad of shiny leaves with a soft layer of fluffy fuzz on the underside.

Each morning Nai Hah Tong gave Phra Phum an offering of rice from the top of the pot. Then he carefully collected the soft fuzz from the underside of the banana leaves and stored it in a pottery jar. His wife, Nang Song Sai, offered Phra Phum flowers and incense. Then she collected the beautiful yellow bananas and sold them at the market.

After three lunar years had passed, Nai Hah Tong had half a kilo of banana fuzz. His wife had three pottery jars full of money. Nai Hah Tong was so busy collecting and storing the fuzz that he paid no attention to his wife's profitable labor. One day Nang Song Sai's father came to ask if he would have to wait much longer for the two kilos of banana fuzz. "I am an old man. If you don't get more land, more banana trees, and more banana fuzz, I shall not live to see copper turned into gold."

"Mai pen rai, don't worry, Father. I will borrow money to buy more land. Then there shall be more banana trees and I can collect even more banana fuzz," said Nai Hah Tong.

Nai Hah Tong and his wife worked for many years. The moons rose, waxed and waned, and days ran after days, until the time arrived when each had accomplished a goal. Nang Song Sai had collected many jars full of money. Nai Hah Tong had two jars full of banana fuzz. Nai Hah Tong shouted to his wife, "Run, run, and bring your father here. Today he can test his magic. If all goes well, we'll see copper glow as golden as the sun of Siam."

When the old man arrived, Nai Hah Tong bowed low before him and gave him the treasured banana fuzz. The old man said: "Arise, my son. Today you will be a rich man."

Nai Hah Tong trembled nervously. Little rivers of perspiration ran down his face. His fingers shook like banana leaves in the wind. The old man, on the other hand, was not in a hurry. He turned to his daughter and calmly asked, "Have you made any money from the sale of bananas?"

"Oh, yes, chai, chai, my father," she said.

Nai Hah Tong thought his father-in-law must be out of his mind. When the copper was waiting to be turned into gold, why worry about the sale of a few bananas?

Nang Song Sai brought in a tray piled high with golden coins and placed it before her husband.

"Aha!" said her father. "Now, Nai Hah Tong, just look at all this money that has been made by following my directions. My son, I cannot turn copper into gold, but you and my daughter have harvested gold from the sale of your bananas. You cared for the young plants until they became trees producing delicious fruit. Is not that just as great a miracle as turning copper into gold?"

Nai Hah Tong did not answer because he felt like a fool, but he was a very rich fool.

His clever wife knelt before him to show her love and respect. When she arose she said, "My husband, you are a master magician. With the help of the gods you cleared land. You cared for the banana trees with the same loving care we give our sons. You made the gods happy, and they rewarded you with the golden fruit of the banana tree."

"Mai chai, that is not right, my clever wife. Do not put a story under your arm and walk away with it. It is your father who is the master magician. He has made his honorable daughter and worthless son-in-law the richest people in Ayudhya."

Nai Hah Tong looked at the meaningless pile of banana fuzz mounted high on the table under the smiling face of his father-in-law. Right there and then, it is said, Nai Hah Tong mixed the banana fuzz with a little water and carefully began to mold it.

"What are you doing?" asked his wife.

"I am making a statue of your father. I hope our sons and our sons' sons will treasure it as a family heirloom. Each time they look upon it, they will be reminded of my foolishness and your father's wisdom."

It is said the statue can be seen in Ayudhya today. It is owned by a wealthy plantation owner who harvests gold, chai . . . gold bananas.

Princess Golden Flower and the Vulture King

One day long ago a favorite wife of King Sanuraj gave birth to a beautiful daughter. When the royal astrologer was consulted regarding the baby's future, he said, "This child is as beautiful as the morning. She smiles as sweetly as a child of the gods but . . . but . . ."

"Chai, chai, yes, yes, go on," said the king impatiently.

"But . . . she will have a very strange habit. She will never be just like other children. However," he added very quickly, "do not despair. The child's unusual habit will save her life one day."

The king replied, "She is a jewel of perfection. We shall guard her well. Perhaps we can prevent this prophecy from coming true."

From that day onward the royal princess was observed carefully. It appeared she was a normal child with no bad habits. She did not suck her thumb. She did not bite her fingernails. She never pointed her toes at the kwan, the spirit that lives in everyone's head. She never forgot to bow properly with hands clasped together. In fact, the child was perfect in every way until she began to speak, and then an unusual thing happened.

Each time the little girl uttered a word, a golden flower fell from her lips. When she sang and danced, the petals fluttered around her and it looked as if she were in a lovely shower of blossom. When she sang herself to sleep, her mat was covered with golden petals. As she played with her cat and called him to her side, rose petals floated in the air. Because of this most unusual characteristic, the king named his daughter Princess Golden Flower.

In spite of her unusual habit it appeared as if the princess would lead a life of happiness. She was the king's favorite daughter, and often she went with her father when he attended festivals. It was easy to recognize her because a little cloud of golden petals always floated about her.

On Kathin Day, the festival that marks the ending of the rains and the first plowing of the rice fields, Princess Golden Flower presented the monks with golden yellow robes. During the Songkran festival, which marks the beginning of the new year, she splashed water on the hands of her parents as a mark of admiration and respect. At the Loy Krathong festival she joined her friends on the banks of the river and made a boat of banana leaves. She said a prayer to the Mother Goddess of the Sea. Then she placed some coins, incense and a lighted candle in the little boat. According to ancient beliefs the little boat carried all her troubles out to sea.

For a long time it seemed as if the astrologer's predictions would not come true. Princess Golden Flower's life had not been in danger. But one day a most frightening thing happened when she was bathing in the river with her attendants. It was almost time to leave when she saw an ugly black vulture devouring the dead body of a dog. She screamed and her attendants screamed too.

The princess was almost faint from the sight and smell of the vulture, but she regained her composure and said calmly, "Come, come, let us leave quickly. The vulture's stench is making me ill. I hope I never see or smell another vulture as long as I live."

Princess Golden Flower returned to the palace, not realizing she had offended the ugly vulture. The bird she had seen was no ordinary vulture: he was the King of the Vultures, a powerful creature who possessed the magic to turn himself into any shape or form.

As the princess and her attendants ran to the palace he hovered above them and cast his black shadow upon them.

"You'll be sorry for insulting me," he said.

The very next day the vulture turned himself into a handsome prince and settled himself in a hut with an old man and his wife. He gave them a chest full of jewels and said, "The treasures in this box are yours, but first you must tell the king I wish to marry Princess Golden Flower."

The old people did as they were told. The king was shocked to hear their strange request. He said, "Guards, find the daring young man who wishes to marry my daughter. Put him in a bag, fill it up with stones, tie it, and throw it in the river."

However, as soon as he said that, he changed his mind and decided to be more lenient. "Tell your young man to build me two bridges, one of pure gold and one of pure silver," he said to the old couple. "The bridges must lead from your hut to the gates of the palace. If they are not completed in twenty-four hours, the young man will be put to death, but if the bridges are completed on time, Golden Flower will be his bride."

The following morning everyone in the entire kingdom was startled to see two bridges leading from a simple hut to the gates of the king's palace. One bridge was made of pure gold and the other was made of pure silver. There was nothing the king could do. A king must keep his word. The very next day, just as the king had promised, the Vulture King married the princess and took her away on a huge black ship.

"Where are we going?" Golden Flower asked.

The Vulture King, still in the form of a handsome prince, did not answer.

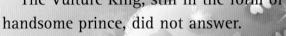

35

Princess Golden Flower trembled as she looked upon the strange, silent crew and smelled the unmistakable odor of vultures. She did not know that every crew member was a vulture in disguise, waiting to destroy her upon a signal from the Vulture King.

When the disguised Vulture King called the crew members into the captain's quarters, Golden Flower seized the opportunity to say a prayer to the Mother Goddess of the Sea. "Please, Mother Goddess, hear my plea. Send someone to rescue me." The princess quickly took a golden flower from her lips and hid it in a silver locket. Then she tied the silver locket to a coconut shell and cast it into the ocean while saying, "May one who is noble chance to see, and have the courage to rescue me." Then Golden Flower heard a splashing sound against the side of the ship. It was the Sea Goddess saying, "Princess Golden Flower, look into the sky. Vultures swarm and vultures fly. Your prince, their king, leads the way. Hide yourself from light of day."

The princess dashed into the hold of the ship and swiftly crawled under a barrel. She huddled there without making a single noise while the vultures swarmed over the decks looking for her. But they could not find her.

Later Princess Golden Flower came out from under the barrel. The seas were calm beneath a clear blue sky. In the distance she saw a graceful white ship. It seemed to be following a frothy white wave that pointed toward her vessel. The princess shouted out happily and hundreds of little golden flowers tumbled into the waves. They floated all around the ship, making a bright ring of gold.

On the approaching ship stood King Pichai, the noble ruler of a mighty kingdom. He held Princess Golden Flower's silver locket in his hand and noticed the flower in the locket matched the flowers in the sea.

"Hurry men, hurry!" he called to his crew. "The princess is in danger."

As he spoke, the sky darkened with the returning cloud of vultures. Luckily, King Pichai was an excellent sailor, and in a few moments he was able to bring his ship close to Golden Flower's ship. He reached the princess's side just as the Vulture King landed on the deck, transformed into a handsome prince holding a sword. At that very instant the noble Pichai plunged his own sword into the Vulture King's heart, killing him instantly.

King Pichai and Princess Golden Flower fell in love at first sight. The Mother Goddess of the Sea returned them safely to King Sanuraj's kingdom where they were happily married.

That year, at the Loy Krathong festival, King Pichai and his bride made a boat from banana leaves. They loaded it with coins, incense, a lighted candle and flowers from Princess Golden Flower's lovely lips. The little boat carried all their worries out to sea.

It is said King Pichai and his beautiful princess lived long and happy lives in a palace scented with the delicate fragrance of golden flowers.

The Wisest Man in Siam

Once long ago, when Thailand was Siam, the country was
ruled by a most powerful man. The mention of his name
made men tremble, women hide, and children as still as
pebbles along the side of the road. As mighty ruler of all Siam, he held
power over life and death in the palm of his hand.

This great king lived a life of luxury. He sat upon a golden throne, slept upon a golden
bed and wore a tiered crown of gold. His royal feet never touched the ground. He hardly
ever walked. Kings in those days used a palanquin, a special kind of chair, in which they
sat proud and tall while servants carried them from one place to another. His food was
served on plates of gold. His clothes were woven from golden thread. Understandably, the
name of this king was "God Over My Head."

The king's servants and guards were tense beyond belief. Their eyes observed each
movement of his hands, for even a small gesture could be a command. Their ears listened
carefully for every word that he might utter. They responded whether he stuttered,
whispered, or spoke in a roar.

Everyone feared the king. The farmers, the hunters, the astrologers too, shared the fear
with the men who trained elephants, the men who made bronze, the men who dug ditches
and created klong canals. The king was, as his name implies, the god over their heads. No
one dared to give advice to him, for he would very easily lose his temper.

Now, far away from the palace wall, there lived a man who wasn't in the least bit
fearful. He was called Sri Tanonchai. Unlike the king, the mention of his name made
people smile and say, "Sri is the wisest man in the land. Sri knows the mystery of sea and
sand. Sri knows all there is to know. He's so smart, he hasn't any foe!" The fame of his
cleverness spread all over the land until he was known simply as Sri of Siam.

This man's memory was incredible. He knew everything by heart. People wore a path to his door as they came to him with their questions. And strange as it may seem, he always knew the right answer.

"Sri, shall I be the father of a boy?" asked a proud young man one day.

"Ah, yes, you shall be the father of a-a-a baby. And if it is not a girl, most certainly it shall be a boy," said Sri with a smile.

Sri lived in a bamboo hut in the shade of a coconut tree on the banks of a lazy brown river. He sat on his haunches, as he had no chair. He slept on a mat on a bare floor. He ate rice and fish and simple curries from a banana leaf plate. His clothes were made of coarse cotton thread. His eyes were sparkling black and bright, and as full of mischief as there is heat in the noontime sun. The fame of Sri reached every corner of the land. One day, the most royal ruler, God Over My Head, overheard his elephant trainer say, "If you don't know the answer, ask Sri. Puzzles, riddles, prophecies, past or future history, recipes, remedies, cures for the cobra's bite or how to dance the ramwong . . . Sri knows everything."

The king stood still and held his breath. "Why, this cannot be. That man speaks as if no one was as smart as Sri. I am the king of my country; never will it be said that a common man has more wit than God Over My Head."

He started out that very day on a mission of revenge. "I'll find Sri, and then we shall see who is smarter!" he said to himself.

He set off proudly on his royal elephant, but he had made sure to dress in a manner quite unlike a king. As a matter of fact, he looked like a king's elephant boy.

After a day, a night, and one more day, the king found his way to the door of the bamboo hut on the river's edge where Sri Tanonchai lived.

The king roared, "Sri of Siam, come here please!"

Sri smiled a big broad grin instead of being cross.

"Sawaddi, good day, good sir. Come and sit down. You appear to have had a very long ride. May I help you in some way?"

The king said, "Sri, I have heard of your fame and I've come to put you to a test."

"There is nothing I like better than a test," said Sri.

"Sri," said the king, "are you as clever as people say?"

"Who knows?" said Sri.

"Not I," said the king. "That is why I am here. I came to find out, one way or another, if you are as clever as our king."

"But how can this be?" asked Sri. "The king has never sent for me. I've never seen the face or heard the voice of King God Over My Head."

"Sri, that problem is easy to solve, because I know the king most intimately and the only person as clever as he — is me! I can tell you with authority. I am his only equal."

"Your elephant has a noble look. No doubt you are one of the king's best. Now, shall we match our wits in a simple contest?" asked Sri.

"Fine," said the king. "We shall match wits today. You must find a way to make me get into the river. You see, I've never liked even the thought of getting wet. Yet, a man who is clever could find a way of enticing me into the water." Sri walked back and forth stroking his chin. There was a sparkle in his eye. He glanced at the river, at the king, and then with a sigh he said, "Good man, you are clever. Clever indeed! I would need magic to make you get in. I guess you win this part of the contest."

40

The king smiled victoriously as Sri continued talking.

"Chai, as much as I want to," he said stroking his chin, "I don't think I could ever make you jump in. But if you were in, and it were my task to make you get out – oh! That would be the ultimate test of my cleverness."

For the king these words of victory were sweet. Without a pause, he leapt from the bank into the muddy river. Sri began to laugh as he heard the king say, "Sri Tanonchai, you won't live another day if you can't get me out of the water at once. Prove how clever you are right now. Prove your wit to the king."

Sri's face was one big smile. "Your Highness, why don't you stay there and think for a while? As far as I'm concerned, you may stay in the water forever if you wish. The river is full of tasty fish, and I'll bring you a dish of rice now and then."

The king looked as if he were going to explode when Sri said, "I won your challenge. There is no doubt. You asked me to make you jump into the river, and there you are."

The king had no more to say. He had been outwitted. He climbed out of the river as lifeless as a broken toy. He nodded to Sri and said, "You are indeed a clever man!"

There Is No Such Thing As a Secret

The king of the country should have been the happiest man in the world. His country was at peace, the paddies produced large quantities of rice, and the royal astrologer predicted great good fortune. To make matters even better, a white elephant had been discovered at the beginning of the king's reign. With all this good fortune the king should have smiled all day long, but to tell the truth — and you should always tell the truth — the king was miserable. He never, ever smiled.

Only one person in the kingdom knew why the king was sad. This man was the king's personal barber. The barber had been sworn to secrecy and he kept the secret very well, so well, in fact, that no one even knew he shared the king's secret.

Each day the king looked more worried and depressed. The people in the court began to talk about their majesty's sad face. Some thought he had a grave illness, but the royal physician said, "He is as healthy as a water buffalo."

Others thought the king was worried about the country becoming poor, but the royal treasurer said, "We have more wealth than the kingdom of China. Our royal treasury has chests full of jewels, our fields are full of rice and our seas are full of fish."

Some said the king's many wives did not love him, but all the royal wives said, "We adore our noble king."

Everyone knew the king had a secret worry, but no one knew what it was.

One day the king's faithful barber became very ill. The king needed a haircut so a substitute barber was found. The new barber was as excited as a monkey with a handful of bananas. He had never served royalty and the thrill of cutting the king's hair was almost more than he could bear. He carefully washed his comb, polished his scissors and wrapped them in a clean white towel. He skipped and sang all the way along the road to the palace.

As soon as the barber arrived, the king himself swore the new barber to secrecy. He said, "You must not tell anyone about anything you might discover today."

The substitute barber had one terrible fault. He could not keep a secret. Everything he did and knew gushed out in a fountain of conversation. The barber was aware of his weakness, but the honor of cutting the king's hair was a rare privilege, so he took the vow and sincerely meant to keep it.

While he was cutting the king's hair, he became aware of something very strange. He said, "Your Majesty, now I know why you are sad. You should not let such a little thing trouble you."

46

"I cannot talk about it," said the king. "Barber, you must keep my secret." The poor barber hurried home with an uncontrollable desire to tell someone about the king's secret. He could not sleep. He could not eat. He refused to talk to anyone. The need to share the secret started to grow like a swelling balloon inside him.

Finally, he could not bear the torture any longer. He hurried from his house and began looking for a lonely place where he could whisper the secret without having anyone hear him. He rowed to the middle of the river, but to his dismay there were fishermen all around him. He walked as far away as he could from the city and wandered on the paths between the rice paddies, but to his dismay there were farmers all around him. He went to the wat, but to his dismay many others had come to the wat and there were people all around him.

The secret was about to burst. The barber was desperate.

He ran as fast as he could for as long as he could and then fell on his face in the tall wet grass. When he had rested for a few moments, he rose to his feet and discovered that he was alone in the king's royal forest. Right beside him was a hollow tree. "This is just the right kind of place. No one can hear me here," he said.

The barber wriggled into the hollow tree and shouted out the secret as loudly as he could. No person heard him, but every grain of wood in the tree absorbed the king's personal secret.

The barber wriggled out of the tree and sighed with relief. He skipped all the way home, feeling as though he was as light as a butterfly and as free as a breeze. It was, indeed, a wonderful day.

Not long after this, the royal drum fell apart. It was very old and had had constant use. Each hour the royal servants had beat the drum to tell the passing of time. If there was anything the palace needed, it was a sturdy drum. The royal drum makers went into the forest and selected a tree with fine wood. By coincidence, the very tree they selected was the barber's hollow tree and every grain of wood in this tree had absorbed the king's personal secret.

The drum makers cut down the tree and had the royal elephant haul it into the courtyard. There they made a beautiful drum.

They carved intricate designs on it and polished it all around. Then they selected the finest oxhide to cover the open end of the drum.

When the palace officials saw it, they said, "Let's invite everyone to see and hear this fine drum. Our king looks so glum. Perhaps the new drum will cheer him up."

The royal astrologers decided upon the proper day for the celebration. All the important people were invited to come. When the great day arrived a huge crowd gathered in the courtyard. Everyone waited expectantly to hear the boom, boom of the new drum, but the new drum did not say, "Boom, boom, boom." The drum said, "The king has moles on his head. The king has moles on his head." It bellowed forth the king's very own personal secret.

A boy in the crowd began to giggle. Other people felt like laughing, but they did not dare to smile. Everybody looked at the king. Now they knew why he had been so worried.

The king frowned and looked very cross. "Bring the substitute barber here," he shouted.

The barber's comb and scissors clicked in his pocket as he stood there trembling in front of the king.

"Barber, did you tell my very own personal secret to the tree?"

The barber nodded and told the truth. You should always tell the truth, you know.

"Release him," said the king. "Let this be a lesson to all of you."

The crowd waited anxiously to hear their king explain. He said, "Do not try to hide a blemish. No one person is perfect, and there is no such thing as a secret."

The great drum roared, "The king has moles on his head. The king has moles on his head."

The king nodded in agreement, and then he began to smile. His eyes began to sparkle and his face was bright with happiness. The king was happy now because he had absolutely nothing to hide. Everybody knew his secret.

How the Tiger Got Its Stripes

Today the tigers in Thailand wear golden fur coats marked with bold black stripes, but the tiger's coat was not always like this. Long ago, the tiger wore a plain golden coat, like a royal robe. As he stalked along the jungle path, the gibbons, the monkeys, the parakeets and the parrots all admired their handsome king. Without a doubt, the tiger was pleased with the style of his coat. As long as he could remember, everyone had always praised him for it. If only he had not met the old man of the jungle, I do believe the tiger would still be wearing a coat of golden fur today.

It all happened one day toward the end of the monsoon season, when the rain fell so hard and so fast that it turned jungle paths into rivers. No one could remember a season that had been as wet as this.

At the time of these great rains, an old man lived near the edge of the dark jungle in a simple bamboo hut placed on posts that were firmly settled in the ground. When the monsoon rains flooded the earth, he was high and dry. At night, when the jungle animals prowled and growled, the old man pulled up his rope ladder and slept soundly. Nothing bothered to come into his house except the little chingchok lizards, of course, and since they ate the mosquitoes, he welcomed them.

All around his hut was a bamboo fence. Within it there had been a vegetable patch, a mango tree, a betel palm, a clump of banana trees and a pond. But now all you could see was a great pool of water and the tops of the trees. The pigs and chickens that had enjoyed the shade under the hut now lived in the house with their master. Each day the old man of the jungle had asked the guardian spirit of his little place to do something about the rain so that things could return to normal.

The guardian spirit must have heard him because one day the rain stopped. The old man was very happy. He climbed down his rope ladder and began to work in his muddy yard. At lunchtime he paused to rest under his coconut tree.

"Ah, there's a nice coconut up there but I could never reach it without a long, strong coconut knife. Since it is such a beautiful day, I think I'll go into the jungle and look for rattan grass. I could trade a few bundles of rattan for a coconut knife."

He said a prayer to the guardian spirit to ask his blessing for the day's adventure and went on his way. A hot sun burned overhead. There were no clouds in the bright blue sky. "I guess the rains are almost over," the old man said.

When he stepped into the jungle he felt the comfortable, refreshing coolness of shade. He smelled the sweet scent of a flowering vine that reached for the sun and cast a tangled shadow on his path. The pulse of a slight breeze seemed to rise and fall with the echoing call of a yellow jungle bird. The old man wandered deep into the center of the jungle before he paused to take a rest.

Suddenly, he felt uneasy. A black shadow had settled all around him. Before he could turn his head to see what it was, a huge golden paw knocked him over. A hot breath blew upon his neck. Then he felt sharp teeth piercing his shoulder. He screamed like a myna bird. The old man of the jungle had been caught by the golden tiger.

The old man thought fast and began to speak rapidly. "Oh, Phra Tiger, honorable tiger, put me down, put me down! Don't eat me!" he yelled.

The tiger tossed the man over and held him under the weight of a heavy front paw.

The tiger roared, "Speak quickly, old man. I'm hungry."

The old man replied, "Eat me if you wish, but if you do, you will be dead by morning."

The tiger said, "Old man, you wrap your tongue around your ears. Did you take a good look at yourself this morning? Did you dip up water with a coconut shell and look at your reflection?"

The old man laughed a little."That I did, Phra Tiger. That I did. I know if you eat me, you will be dead by morning!"

The tiger growled and shook his head. "Explain yourself!" he roared.

"Phra Tiger, honorable tiger, if you free me, I could tie you to the top of a tree with heavy ropes of rattan."

"Now why would you want to do a silly thing like that?" said the tiger.

"Haven't you heard? A great rain will flood our jungle this evening. All the village men are busy building rafts. I came to pick rattan so they could tie their logs together."

The hard gleam in the tiger's eye began to soften a little. "Phra Tiger, you might fall from the top of a tree. Perhaps I could build a raft for you and tie you to it. Then you would float safely on top of the floodwater instead of being drowned by it."

"Hummmrum," growled the tiger.

"Free me, Phra Tiger. If I don't start building your raft now, it won't be ready in time."

"I'll free you," said the tiger, "but don't try to escape or I'll swallow you in one gulp."

The old man did not try to get away. He quickly gathered sturdy rattan grass and twined it into a rope. He used the rope to tie some logs together to make a raft that was just big enough to hold the enormous tiger.

"Hurry, Phra Tiger," he called. "There isn't much time before the sky darkens and the rain clouds burst."

The tiger lay on the raft and growled, "Tie me securely now. Don't do a careless job."

"Chai, chai, yes, yes, Phra Tiger," the old man said.

As the old man tied the last knot, securely binding the tiger to the raft, he smiled and said, "You are a lucky tiger. No matter how much it rains, you will be safe."

The tiger purred like a contented house cat. The old man placed both his hands together, bowed low before the captured tiger, and said politely, "Sawaddi, good day, Phra Tiger."

That night the sky darkened, but it did not rain. The next day it did not rain either. The poor tiger was hungry and very sleepy. As each hour passed, he grew angrier and angrier. When two rising suns had burned the mist off two mornings, the tiger knew the old man had tricked him.

The tiger wriggled and squirmed, twisted and turned. With each movement he made, the slender rattan ropes cut more deeply into his beautiful golden coat. Finally, with a savage, desperate surge of energy he freed himself from the rattan ties that had bound him up.

Oh, he was a ragged-looking tiger. His beautiful golden coat was ripped and slashed where the rattan had held him to the raft.

The tiger never recovered from the old man's trick. He repaired his coat but he could not hide the black slashes where his fur had been sewn back together. From that day on, the tiger of Thailand has worn a golden coat striped with the bold black scars of his unfortunate meeting with the old man of the jungle.

As for the old man, he decided to get along without the long-handled coconut knife. "After all," he said, "there are more important things in life than coconuts."

The Footprint of the Buddha

Many years ago there was a group of young Buddhist monks who lived in a temple in Siam. They decided to make a religious pilgrimage to the footprint of Buddha on the crest of Adam's Mountain in Ceylon. The great father of their wat warned the young monks to be careful. "The journey to Ceylon is dangerous," he said. "Snakes, crocodiles and tigers will cross your path."

"We are not afraid. We believe in Buddha's goodness," they answered. "Look, our legs are as sturdy as the branches on the teak tree. Our faith and our feet will carry us through the jungles to the true footprint of Buddha."

Their departure was a beautiful sight to see. The monks' golden robes gleamed in the sunlight and fluttered like banners in the tropical breeze. The very grass they stepped upon seemed to glitter green with the touch of their bare feet. The elder monks beat the gongs in the wat and the metallic booms resounded with a pulsing rhythm, announcing to everyone that the young brothers of the priesthood were beginning a holy journey.

Each morning the monks woke before dawn and walked from village to village. The farmers gave them food most willingly, for they gained religious merit by placing a serving of rice in the monks' bowls. Day ran after day and finally the monks reached their destination, the shrine of the sacred footprint in Ceylon. The Ceylonese monks were surprised to see their brothers from Siam. "Were you not afraid to travel all alone in the jungle?" they asked.

"We were not afraid. We believed in Buddha's goodness," they answered.

The monks from Siam placed red, white and yellow flowers before the shrine of the footprint. Near the flowers they lighted sticks of incense, making the air sweet and heavy with delicate fragrance. As they said prayers of thankfulness, they bowed low and kissed the sacred earth where Buddha had once stood.

When they arose the Ceylonese monks said, "Why have you come here to worship our footprint of Buddha? Our ancient scriptures tell us there is a footprint of Buddha located upon the Golden Hill in your country."

The Siamese monks doubted this. "It cannot be true."

The Ceylonese monks said, "Our ancient scriptures prove our words. Look, the holy writing on the dried palm leaves tells of a footprint of Buddha on the Golden Hill in Siam."

The Siamese monks hurried home so fast that at times their golden robes seemed like fluttering wings of birds floating through the jungle. They told King Song Dharm about their miraculous discovery.

The king was very happy and immediately began the search for the footprint of Buddha.

58

The king's men looked on Golden
Hill and on all the mountains and
in every valley, but they could not
find the footprint.

Day ran after day. The grasses grew
tall in the tropical sun. The trees stretched
their limbs to greater heights. The river flowed
into an ebbing sea and the ancient country of Siam grew
older with each setting of the red-tinted sun. The young
monks who had made the long journey to Ceylon
were now the great fathers of their wat. Their
brown bodies were as wrinkled as
the withered palm leaves that told
of Buddha's footprint. Their voices
were a faint whisper now, but
they never stopped talking about
the footprint. "It is lost like a ruby in a
basket of rice. We must sift each grain to find
our country's lost treasure."

Some people doubted and accused the monks of hearing
a story, tucking it under their arm and walking away with
it, which is a Siamese way of saying the story is not true. Although
many doubted, the monks said every day, "We will find the
footprint. Believe in Buddha's goodness."

Their faith was rewarded, for one day a farmer ran into their wat
shouting like a dancer at a rice festival, "Boon found it! Boon found
the footprint of Buddha. Come to Saraburi. Hurry, he is going to tell
us how it happened!"

The old monks hobbled as fast as their bare feet and aged limbs could carry them. When they arrived in Saraburi, they found the hunter, Boon, in the market square with a crowd of curious people gathered around him. As Boon began to speak, the crowd hushed. The old monks leaned forward to hear each word.

Boon said, "I was hunting a small spotted deer with my crossbow on Golden Hill. The deer paused for a moment, I aimed, and let my bamboo arrow fly. It pierced the flesh, and blood ran from the wound like tears of death. The deer didn't fall to the ground. He limped into a thicket of tall green grass. I ran after him, but

before I could catch up with him, he bounded from the grass as though he'd never been wounded. I was even more surprised when I saw that my arrow was not in his side and his wound was gone.

"I followed the spots of red upon the earth. They led me to a pool of clear water. It was like a sapphire glittering in the sun. All around it the moss curled rich and green. The deer's footprints stopped by the little pool. I thought the deer must have stopped to drink so I, too, paused to drink some of the water. One swallow of the water cooled my body and made me feel as clean as a white lotus.

"Suddenly, I felt very well. All my life I have had pain in my arms, but the pain disappeared and I felt as strong as an elephant pulling teak logs.

"I was dizzy with delight. I splashed in the pool until all the water had spilled out onto the ground. There, at the bottom, I found the imprint of a human foot. It is the footprint of our Lord Buddha."

The monks' hearts beat faster with every word Boon uttered. The light of contentment gleamed in their eyes. It is said they climbed the Golden Hill with a determined stride like the young monks of old who had climbed Adam's Mountain in Ceylon. Their lips uttered the prayers of thankfulness that overflowed from their hearts.

People still speak of the great surge of joy that filled the hearts of everyone in old Siam on that wonderful day long ago. From that day to this, the footprint of Buddha has been a sacred treasure. It reminds everyone of Buddha's faith in the goodness of man.

Glossary

chai   yes; that is right

chingchok   a small lizard found in Southeast Asia

chula   the name given to the male kite in the Thai sport of kite fighting. The chula is a large, star-shaped kite with five points. It is flown on a long string.

Kathin   a holiday honoring Buddhist monks, held after the rain season and the plowing of the rice fields

klong   canals that serve as water roads, providing arteries for travel and transportation in cities and in the countryside

kwan   the personal spirit residing in the head; a being responsible for health, wealth and general comfort

mai chai   no; that is not right

mai pen rai   never mind; it doesn't matter; don't worry

mai ruu   I don't know

namprik	a pungent, spicy sauce made from a carefully blended mixture of seasonings, water and a small black beetle that the Thais call maengda
pai	go now
pakpao	the name given to the female kite in the Thai sport of kite fighting. The pakpao is a small, dainty kite with a long tail. It is frequently made in the shape of a diamond.
Phra	an honorary title, meaning "sacred one" or "honored one"
Phra Phum	the sacred spirit of a Thai dwelling, meaning "the spirit of the place"
ramwong	a graceful Thai folk dance
rawang	be careful; watch what you are doing; observe closely
Siam	the old name for Thailand
sawaddi	hello; how do you do; goodbye
wat	a Buddhist temple

ABOUT TUTTLE
"Books to Span the East and West"

Our core mission at Tuttle Publishing is to create books which bring people together one page at a time. Tuttle was founded in 1832 in the small New England town of Rutland, Vermont (USA). Our fundamental values remain as strong today as they were then—to publish best-in-class books informing the English-speaking world about the countries and peoples of Asia. The world has become a smaller place today and Asia's economic, cultural and political influence has expanded, yet the need for meaningful dialogue and information about this diverse region has never been greater. Since 1948, Tuttle has been a leader in publishing books on the cultures, arts, cuisines, languages and literatures of Asia. Our authors and photographers have won numerous awards and Tuttle has published thousands of books on subjects ranging from martial arts to paper crafts. We welcome you to explore the wealth of information available on Asia at **www.tuttlepublishing.com**.

Published by Tuttle Publishing, an imprint of Periplus Editions (HK) Ltd.

www.tuttlepublishing.com

Text Copyright © 2019 Marian D. Toth
Illustrations © 2019 Patcharee Meesukhon

Library of Congress Control Number in progress
ISBN 978-0-8048-3708-8

Distributed by:

North America, Latin America and Europe
Tuttle Publishing, 364 Innovation Drive
North Clarendon, VT 05759-9436
Tel: 1 (802) 773 8930
Fax: 1 (802) 773 6993
info@tuttlepublishing.com
www.tuttlepublishing.com

Asia Pacific
Berkeley Books Pte Ltd
3 Kallang Sector #04-01
Singapore 349278
Tel: (65) 6741 2178
Fax: (65) 6741 2179
inquiries@periplus.com.sg

22 21 20 19   8 7 6 5 4 3 2 1   Printed in Hong Kong   1903EP